The Vikings,
Facts or Fictions

by
Bo Widerberg

The Vikings came originally from the three
Scandinavian countries, Sweden, Norway and
Denmark. These ferocious sea-farer traveled far in
their open longboat. They visited Iceland, North
America, and Greenland.

They were also in England, Ireland, and at
Normandy France. We have three of our week-days
named after them, Wednesday, Thursday and
Friday are named after the famous Vikings, Odin,
Thor, and Odin's wife Freya.

The Vikings were traders, but they were also
skilled craftsmen as blacksmiths, and metalwork.
They were also farmers, fishermen and trappers.
Many of them settled in Russia, Iceland, Greenland
and North America, even as far away as part of
Asia.

You can find that many of the Viking's, settled in

Ireland, and they established towns along the Irish west coast, like Dublin, which the Vikings started building 841 AD. Then also Wexford, Cork and Limerick. These new towns meant that trade between Ireland and England, and even trade with Europe, develop faster, partly because of the Vikings.

The Vikings that lived in Denmark, or Norway, traveled south and west with their longboats. To England, Scotland, Ireland and France, even across the Atlantic, to Iceland, Greenland and North America. From Sweden the Vikings went east, to Finland, Russia, the Baltic states, Poland, Germany and even as far as part of Asia.

The word Viking comes from an old English word, 'wicing' at the time it stood for 'Pirate.'. The name was changed to Viking, to make their name sound better to the public. It unfortunately didn't help much, to give the Vikings a better reputation. Mostly because they were a bunch of fighting savages, and were always in trouble. Or, if they couldn't find any trouble, the once from Asgard were good at starting trouble themselves.

Many of the Vikings in Ireland, married Irish citizens and they became known as Irish-Norse. However, the Vikings and the people that lived on

Ireland didn't always agree, and continued to fight each other. Sometime an Irish King would join with a Viking leader, to attack another Irish Chief, or King. Warfare was because of this common at that time. One of the worse, but unfortunate true stories about the Vikings, they did take and sold slaves, both male and female. Although some of them were what you would call anti-social, there were also good Vikings. Their time in history, was between 800 AD., and 1100 AD.

A great battle, known as the battle of Clontarf, took place year 1014 just outside Dublin, on Ireland's west coast. At Clontarf, the strongest King of Ireland at the time, the Irish High King Brian Boru, fought and defeated a Viking army. After this battle, peace started to develop between the Vikings and the Celtic people, and they gradually adopted each other's ideas and customs.

We know all this about the Vikings because they buried items like jewelry, tools, weapons and household goods in their graves. Sometimes an entire ship was buried with an important person.

The Vikings also settled in parts of England and in the region of France now called Normandy. That name came from the fact that most Vikings traveling south, were called Norsemen, and so the name Normandy.

When Odin became a God, he with his wife Freya lived at Valhalla where the other two members of Odin's family lived. It was there his sons Thor and Loki lived together with their parents Odin and his wife Freya. They were all well over six feet tall, and stronger than most Vikings. However, before Odin became a God, he was a normal Viking himself, as the rest of them. Odin married Freya, and they had a son, Thor. The trouble started when Loki became jealous of Thor. Loki was a younger son of Odin. "Give me a hammer like the one you gave Thor, he demanded from Odin, and I'll change the world to suit us, not the other way around. Loki said in a demanding voice. Valhalla was where the Gods lived, Odin with his family lived there. Most of the other Vikings lived at a place called Asgard. That was where the Vikings army was located, and where most of what you would call the anti-social Vikings resided.

Loki, didn't have any success with Odin. He never got to use the hammer. So, he decided to find his own way in the world, down among the regular people. He would lose some of his strength. However, as he was six feet six inches tall, of well-developed muscles, he did well anyway. As all this happened around 800 years after the married couple Joseph and Maria gave birth to their son Jesus, down in the near East. The world had changed some. Most of the happenings were now in Europe, and in old England of course. We shouldn't forget Ireland, and the Belfast area where the Vikings made several towns, Belfast included as one of them.

Loki, started to spend more and more time around the regular people down on the planet, as he had decided to leave Valhalla for good. If I don't get a hammer they can keep it, was his thoughts. He, one day met this good-looking woman as he was spending a day at a market place, just looking around. Her father, he later found out was the towns blacksmith, and she lived as comfortable as Loki did himself. When he told her how well he thought she looked and that he himself was part of

Odin's family and the gang up in Valhalla. She threw her arms around his neck, and tried to get him to follow her to her father. "You have to meet my dad," she said in her sweetest voice, trying hard to pull Loki along.

Loki, was as Thor, a big man. A good six feet six inches tall. Light brown, almost blond hair, and a good beard. Clear blue eyes and a strong body. He had broad shoulders, and a narrow waist. He dressed like most well to do people did at that time.

"Hold on my woman, why are we in such a hurry? I don't even know your name." said Loki strongly effected by her good looks. "I don't mind meeting your father, or your family, my lass. However, to do that I need to know your name, and where you live, by the way my own name is Loki.

"Well I am Helga. Or, Helga Bjornhild, if you need all of it. Now when that is settled, let's go and see my father right away," said Helga as she grabbed a good hold of Loki's arm and tried to drag him along. "It is behind those market tables over there." She added a she pointed the way. She was dressed like most maidens, in a woman's cotton dress of bright colors. However, she had a glorious body that the plain dress couldn't hide, and a beautiful face to go with it.

"Is it far away?" said Loki, not understanding this woman. "Why is she in such a hurry," he thought as he slowly started to follow her to her father Bjornhild.

"No, it is not far at all. Just on the other side of this market, not far at all. You can see it from here," she said as she pointed the way and tried her best to drag Loki along, a little bit faster.

Helga had at last got Loki up to the towns blacksmith, her father. Loki was greatly impressed by the size of the workshop. "My father's name is Trygg and he would like to meet you Loki. Please come now, it isn't dangerous, my father is a nice old gentleman, and he wouldn't hurt a fly."

Trygg Bjornhild, is a strong man, medium tall and being the town's only blacksmith, he had developed strong muscles all over. He is an inch under six feet, and he doesn't have much hair left on his head, but an enormous beard that is tied together behind his neck, not to interfere with his work.

"Mr. Trygg, I met your daughter Helga down by the market, and she wanted me to come here to see you sir, so I followed her as she asked me to do."

"Have they given you a name my young man? Mine is Trygg Bjornhild." Said the blacksmith without looking up from his work.

"But Dad!" answered Helga. "He is living with Odin, Thor, and Freya up in Valhalla. He is part of their family dad. If I searched for the rest of my life, I couldn't find a better man than this Loki," added Helga to get her father's interest."

"Have you ever seen the Dragon, Nidhug?" said Trygg Bjornhild as he was looking up at Loki, not giving Helga a glance.

"No Sir, Bjornhild, I haven't seen our dragon Nidhug. To see that dragon, and to be eaten by the dragon Nidhug, you must be dead. She eats only dead Vikings. And Sir Bjornhild as you can see, I'm still alive, and a young man." Said Loki to Helga's father.

"I knew that, I only wanted to check up on you, to see if you knew anything about the Vikings Dragon. Now, I have finished a sword for a customer living not too far away. It is for a gentleman, Sir Count Drake, a good customer of mine. Would it be asking too much, if I asked you Loki and my daughter Helga to deliver this sword to my customer? You can of course use my own horse for the trip. Helga knows where my customer Count Drake lives."

"That would be my pleasure Sir Bjornhild. When would you like us to start?" said Loki, his head full of this talkative but good-looking maiden Helga.

As Helga knew what had to be done, she took Loki out to the stable, and said. "We can have two fast horses, and be back here with father, later today. Or we can use the old work horse, and be back late tomorrow. It is your choice Loki."

"I have a feeling that one horse should be enough for the two of us, if it is used to carry two people." He said with all his thoughts around this young maiden, and didn't even give the sword a second thought.

"Yes Loki, it is strong enough to carry three heavy men. The two of us weigh only enough for one heavy person. We have no problem with this horse, and we call him Acer." She said as she started to talk slowly to the horse. Loki could see how the horse moved his ears, listened to her, and felt fully relaxed by the soft voice the horse recognized.

Holding the sword, the blacksmith Trygg had

made, in his hands, Loki looked as Helga used a large box to get up on this big horse, that she straddled without a saddle. "Come up here Loki, climb up on this box first, then up in front of me. Could you give me the sword first?" she said as she took a good hold of this beautiful sword her father had made for one of his customers, Count Drake.

Against all odds, Loki came up on Acer. He was sitting behind Helga to be able to hold his arm around her waist, and he was pressing her against his chest as she kept talking to the horse, keeping the animal fully relaxed.

On the way to her father's customer, they had to pass a small forest. Inside this forest three criminally minded young men were waiting for some people to come by, so they could rob them. And as they only had one sword between them, they were looking for an easy target. The three friends, Ralph, Sam and Phil, had been hiding in the bushes of this forest for a good hour, with not a single person, or a horse coming down the trail.

The only other alternative, would be working at the tavern, and these three would do anything to get away from working in the tavern, they all shuddered at the thought. They had only one old sword between them. Sam and Ralph kept their eyes on the dirt road passing by this forest, while Phil was quietly talking to their horses, to keep them relaxed. Then they saw this big horse coming their way carrying two people.

"That horse coming our way will help us with today's finance, if we do it the right way," said Sam as he added, "My turn with the sword Ralph. You had it with our last people we robbed. You did a good job Ralph, but now it is my turn. However, at that time they were four people riding on four horses, but we took their money anyway, didn't we?" Sam said with a glee.

"Yeah, Sam you are right there. I had four people, and we took care of all their money, didn't we? But you are right, here is the sword Sam. It is your turn. And boys," added Ralph, "If we don't get enough money together, we will have to help that awful woman Gertrud back at her tavern. When we get some money together, I thought it might be a good idea to buy another sword, or maybe two."

"A good idea," said Sam. "We would look more

sinister. And it would make our customer to empty their purses quicker." Agreed Sam.

Both Sam and Ralph are of normal height for a man. Both with large beard, and both their hair, and their beard, was as usual tied behind their neck. The third one of them, Phil, was slightly smaller, maybe five feet seven inches. However, he had the same hair and eye colors. They were all three dressed in heavy work clothing's, and large work boots on their feet's. The only way to dress when you are in the forest.

"Well, Sam, as I took care of the last customer I agree that now it's your turn." Said Ralph again, and with those words he gave Sam the old sword, the only sword these three had between them. And Sam jumped up on his horse while the other two left their horses in the forest, as they were expecting to be pick up the money and jewelry from the ground.

"What about me!" said Phil in too loud a voice. "Even if I'm shorter than you guys, I'm as good with the sword as any of the two of you. It isn't right that you two should have all the fun. And, if it hadn't been for me and Sam, we wouldn't have had a dime from those four people, and you know that Ralph," Said Phil, the smallest of the bandits as they all had their eyes on this big horse coming closer, carrying two people.

"Yeah, Phil, for the next person that willingly give us his money, you will have the sword," said Ralph as they now concentrated on this big horse with two people. "And If you keep talking with a loud voice Phil, you'll tell these people we are here." Said Sam, as they made themselves ready to relieve this people from their money.

"Well it should have been my turn with the sword." Said Phil having a hard time keeping his voice down. "You two are keeping the sword as your own property. I'm a member of our group, aren't I? And I should be treated as such." Insisted Phil as he with a sullen look waited for this huge horse to come closer.

"Of course, you are a member of our team. However, Phil as we haven't got more than one sword and I have had my turn now it is Sam's turn. The next one, will be yours." Said Ralph as he looked at Sam that was holding the sword. "Is that okay with you Phil?"

The three bandits, with their heads covered with hoods, came out of the forest. Sam sat on his horse, while Phil and Ralph stood on the road, and they all stopped in front of Acer, blocking his way. Sam, the one of them with the sword, had it already drawn as he looked at Loki and Helga. And with a strong voice, he demanded. "We need your money and your jewelry, good people. Please put it down in front of my friends, or take the consequences." Said Sam as he lifted the old sword in a threatening way above his head, while Ralph and Phil that had left their horses in the forest were standing on the road, where they were waiting for the money to be thrown down on the ground as usual, close to where they were standing.

As Loki had to turn some to be able to see the man with the sword better, he took the sword from Helga, and with a jump he was down from Acer. He looked at the young man with the sword, that now had the sword pointing right at Loki. Loki without saying a word, and with one sweep of the new sword, had cut the hand of the surprised man that had been holding the sword. With a scream of pain, Sam fell of his horse, on to the ground. Loki turned to the other two, and said in a soft and calm voice. "Take a cloth and tie it around your friend's arm, or he will die from loss of blood." Then he moved his sword around to be sure the other two didn't try to pick up Sam's sword with his right hand still firmly attached to it. The two bandits didn't even look at the sword, they only helped their hand-less friend, and his horse back in to the forest, where the other two horses were waiting.

"Was I in luck this time" thought Phil, "that it wasn't my turn to have the sword. Sam's going to have some big problem with Gertrud down at the tavern, with only one hand. He was always in trouble when he had two hands." thought Phil as he smiled within himself. He didn't for a second give Sam's pain a thought that he might be in great pain, now when he lost his right hand.

"That was a very fast move you did with the sword Loki, cutting of his hand like that, while he was sitting on his horse," said Helga. "Where did you learn how to handle a big sword like this one?"

"It's a family thing." Said Loki. "All of us up at Valhalla knows how to take care of ourselves, and our friends." Loki added as he with a jump was back up on Acer. "Now my good woman, is there a town close by, that we can pass on the way to deliver this sword to your father's customer? I would like a tumbler of good ale, and maybe a bed for an hour or two to get away from the hottest part of the day."

With her cheeks redder than usual, she with a whisper told Loki that behind this small forest, on the south side, is a small town that has a good tavern. "It wouldn't add more than an hour to our journey, at the most." She said as she pressed herself closer to Loki.

Turning Acer that way, they could behind the forest see the first homestead of this town. Helga said something to Acer in a quiet voice, and the horse walked past all the other homesteads, and walked right up to the tavern, and its stable. Like he knew the way, and had been there several times before.

"I can see that Acer has been here before," said Loki with a smile as he grabbed Helga's waist, and helped her down from Acer. "If you know the people in this tavern Helga, it might be better if you ask for some cold ale, when we enter the tavern."

As they entered the tavern through a big solid wooden door, the first person they saw, was the hand-less bandit, and his two friends that had carried him inside. "We were attacked by some strangers, and one of them cut of Sam's hand for no reason at all." Said the shorter one of the two.

"That was a dirty lie," said Helga in a firm and loud voice that was heard well, as they entered the tavern. "We came from my father's black-smith foundry in Main Town, to deliver a sword he has made for Count Drake, further to the east. When we were to pass the small forest close by, these three attacked us and demanded our money and our jewelry. My partner Loki defended us, and cut of Sam's hand. That is the truth, and let Thor's hammer hit me if that wasn't the entire truth." Said Helga as she with a dirty look turned herself away from the whining robbers.

"My dear Lady, of course we believe you." Said one of the customers. "These three has never amounted to anything, and now when they tried their wits as thieves and robbers, even that was a failure." Said this stout woman, that was nicely dressed, and she had her long black hair in a big knot on top of her head. She was sitting by one of the tables, enjoying her ale together with a lady friend. "Please sit down, and enjoy yourself with a tumbler of ale. I would be happy to pay for your drinks. We have for such a long time been hoping that these three would find something they could do, or be good at. And what I can see, they haven't found it yet. May I ask for your names? Mine is Gertrud, and my friend here is Astrid."

"Of course, you may Gertrud, mine is Helga Bjornhild, and my protective friend is Loki, from Valhalla."

"Do we have a member of the Gods among us?" said Gertrud as she with a smile that covered her round face looked at Loki. "You my Sir Loki are you from Valhalla, or are you from Asgard?"

"Gertrud, my good woman," said Loki, "I am, as my family from Valhalla. And my friend here, Helga Bjornhild, as I hope will be a longtime friend of mine. Is from the big market at Main Town, where her father is the towns blacksmith. He has made this beautiful sword that his daughter and I are to deliver to one of his customers, a Count Drake, living not too far from here I have been told."

"We all know the Count well, and he happens to be here at my tavern today. I'll call him down, so you can have your business together." With those words, Gertrude with her walking stick hit the ceiling of the tavern a few times, and in only a minute some heavy steps could be heard as the Count came down from the upper floor.

As he recognized Helga right away, he also saw the sword Loki was holding. "Has that father of yours finished my sword already?" he said with a smile that covered his entire face. Then taking the sword from Loki that was holding the sword, he looked at Helga again. "This must be the most beautiful sword he has ever made. Has it been tested?"

Count Drake, is an elderly man of good standing, he is dressed in what is demanded of a citizen of his standing. He is almost bald, but with a long beard down to his chest, and a big mustache. The beard had been black once, but now it had a silvery color, same with the mustache.

"Yes, Count Drake. On our way here, we were stopped by three criminals. They said they needed our money, and our jewelry. However, my new friend here, Loki, using your sword my Count made them change their mind. Those three are well known here in this town, and in this tavern. Someone here should be able to tell you who they are. And Count Drake, one of them lost one of his hands to your new sword. However, that person is still alive, and the people here in the tavern knows who he is, and where he is," Said Helga as she and Loki lifted their tumbler of ale, towards the Count, and enjoyed a big gulp of Gertrude's good ale

Gertrud for a while looked at the Count, then she said. "If this is something you would like to take care of Count Drake, we will of course take him to your estate for you do what you feel is right. We have him hidden away, with only one hand, he is totally useless. Even when he had two hands, we couldn't find anything he was able to do in a satisfactory manner."

"No, my dear Gertrud. I have no interest in that young man. Leave him where he is, and let's forget about him." Said Count Drake as he stood up ready to leave with his entourage, and his new sword of course. Holding the sword in his hand, he looked at Helga, "Tell your father thanks for a well-done job. To give me such a good weapon, I might have to order more swords from him."

The two young criminals that were left, Ralph, and Phil, couldn't decide what to do now without their third member, Sam. "We tried to rob people, it didn't work out too well. Now when there are only two of us, what can we do?" said Ralph looking at his smaller friend Phil. "Do you have any ideas, or any suggestions? Anything you can think of?"

"Well, Ralph," said Phil. "We haven't tried trading at our local market. I have snatched away a lot of items over the years, all of it from Main Town. I'm sure most of it could be sold here at our own towns market tables. When we get low in stock, we just steal some more saleable products. Not from around here though. We have to ride up to Main Town and steal from there, so the people that buy from our own market table doesn't recognize their own stuff."

"Should be a workable idea, I like it," said Ralph. "I have amassed some stuff myself over the years, as you said. And to steal some more from Main Town shouldn't be any problem as I can see it. Yeah, Phil let's put our stuff together, and find out what we have."

When the two young hoodlums put all their stolen items together, they were both surprised how much they had, and how many good saleable, almost new items they had between them. "This will work out fine," said Ralph as he with a proud smile looked at it all. "Now, we do have another problem, that has to be solved. How do we get a table at the market? There ought to be someone we can share a table with, and give them part of our profit. Let's get up to the market, and check it out." The two put all their stolen items in a cart, and as they didn't like too much work, they used one horse to pull it up towards the market place.

Leaving the horse at a stable, they both pulled the cart closer to the market tables, "I don't know anyone personally. We'll have to walk around the market area, and find one that isn't selling too well, or have space on their own table. That person might like to get some of our profit." Said Phil as he started to look around the market area for a possible partner.

Then they both saw this elderly man, sitting on his chair looking dead bored. He looked like he had seen better days, and he didn't have many products on his table either, so Phil walked up and said. "Hello old man, my friend here and I need some space here at the market. Would you mind if we put our stuff here on your table? We would pay you ten percent of what we sold of our own stuff. Is that okay with you? By the way, I'm Phil, and my friend here is Ralph. Nice to meet you my friend."

The old man looked at the two for a while, then he put his hand out, and said. "I am Orvald, nice to meet you partner. Would you accept twenty percent of what you sold from my table?"

Orvald is a man around the mid-fifties. Looking old for his age, but still moveable, and he is dressed in the usual heavy cotton clothing most men around here are wearing.

"Sure Orvald, it's a deal. Can we start to put up some of our stuff right away? Or, do we need to get permission from someone?" said Phil, as both he and Bruce started to put up the better items they had stolen, and had with them in the cart, on Orvald's table.

"No permissions needed, I am the owner of this market." Said Orvald with what could have been a smile. "Bring all your products, put them here on my table, and start selling. By the way boys, I also own the large stable, and the feed store for all kinds of animals." Added Orvald as he with satisfaction looked at some of the items Phil and Ralph had put up on his table.

Phil looked at Ralph, and said. "Let's get some more of our stuff from the wagon." On the way, there he quietly asked Ralph what he thought about this Orvald.

"He should be our next target. Owning the market, the stable and also the feed store for all animals. He must have a lot of money that should belong to us." Said Ralph as he helped Phil with the stolen items.

"My thoughts as well," said Phil as he put more of the stolen merchandise on a trolley and started back to Orvald's table, for hopefully a good day of selling.

Now when Count Drake had the sword Helga's father, Trygg Bjornhild, had made, he with his entourage was about to start his journey home to his estate. Then looking at Helga, he said, "I need another sword, and I have two old swords that your father Trygg could use, and maybe he could make one good sword out of the two. Would it be a good time for the two of you to follow me to my home, so I could give you the swords, your father will have to use to make a new one?"

"Count Drake, it would be an honor for us to be able to join you on your way home. We do have our own horse, old Acer." Said Helga with her best curtsey.

The Count accepted her gracious behavior, looked at the innkeeper and said, "May we borrow an extra horse for this young couple?"

"But of cause Count Drake. Our horse Belinda knows this stallion Acer, and is calm together with that old stallion." Looking at one of his young helper, he told the young boy to get Belinda quickly for the Count.

As the young boy quickly came back with the horse, Loki let Helga ride on Belinda, as he himself jumped up on the large Acer. With a smile, he looked at the Count, "We are ready Count Drake, should I follow in the rear?"

"As I understand it Loki, you are part of Odin and Freya up at Valhalla. Come up here my friend and ride beside myself, and my good friend's daughter Helga."

The entire entourage had ridden for an hour and some when many Vikings, well-armed with swords and axe's, came riding on horses, dressed and behaving like marauding Vikings. Two of the first once drew their swords, and in a rude way told the Count, "We need your money, and be quick about it. Or, if you prefer, we can of course dig it out ourselves from your dead body."

Loki leaned over towards the Count, and in a low voice he asked if he could borrow the new sword for a short while. The Count without making too many movements let the sword come closer to Loki. He immediately looked at the talkative one of the group of these marauding Vikings, and with the sword in his hand he jumped down from Acer, and said. "In the name of Valhalla, I will give you my good men, one chance to ride away, and forget you ever saw us, in that way you will keep on living. Or, if you prefer to stand and fight, Vikings, if that is what you choose, I am at your service." As Loki said this, he made a gracious bow toward the two Vikings that were holding their swords and battle axe's ready.

The talkative one of these two Vikings jumped of his horse, and threw himself at Loki, with his sword well above his head, ready to split Loki in half. Before anyone could see any movements at all, Loki had decapitated the criminal, and with the Viking's head lying on the ground, Loki looked at the other twenty odd Vikings. "Any more of you my good men, that are in need of some exercise?" Before any of the Vikings had a chance to answer, there was a tremendous thunder shaking the entire area. Then a loud voice, they all could hear clearly, said. "Having some exercise my brother. That was a good, and fast move you did. I'm sure that not many of the regular people down there did even see your move. Well, all of us up here saw your move Loki, and your father send his regard, he also said he accept this girl Helga, if she has a place in your heart."

"What was that? Said Count Drake looking at tad pale, and with a worried look, moved closer to Loki.

"It was my brother Thor," said Loki, and with a smile he looked at Helga. "Did you hear what Odin had said?"

"Yes, Loki, I did hear it, every word of it. And, my whole heart feels happy." Looking up to the sky, she added, "Thank you all."

The normally talkative Count Drake, was quiet for a good while, then he said. "If Thor, is your brother, who then are your parents?"

"My father's name is Odin, and my mother is his wife Freya and you all heard my brother Thor. I am from Valhalla as the rest of my family. Well Sir Drake, my father Odin was not a God at the time we were born. He became a God sometime later in our life. I have chosen to live with you people, instead of living up at Valhalla. A decision I'm proud of, and because of that decision, I was lucky enough to meet my Helga Bjornhild."

"This is an enormous event. You are not supposed to be riding with me, I am the one that should be down on my knees in front of you, Sir Loki." Said Count Drake as he tried to dismount his horse to give his reverence to Luke.

"Please Count Drake. When I chose to live down here together with your mortal people, I lost the power I had up at Valhalla. I am now only an ordinary man. I may live a few years longer than most of you. However, I haven't even got a family name. When we live together Helga and I, I'll have to use my wife's name Bjornhild. Not even my brother Thor, has a family name."

At that time, the air echoed again with Thor's voice. "That is true my brother. I must ask Odin why? I'll let you know his answer when I find it out. We should have a family name, shouldn't we?" Said Thor, and it took only some minutes, and Thor's voice was back again, and we all could hear his strong voice. "It seems like we do have a family name Loki, Odin told me it is 'Ragnarok'."

The Vikings had quickly disappeared when they heard Thor's voice. Not one of them left to fight.

Phil and Ralph, with all their stolen items, did well at Orvald's table. As Orvald had more experience with products, and prices, the two let Orvald tell the customer the price of all products on the table, even their own stolen stuff. And after giving him his twenty percent, they still had more money left than they ever had in their young lives. With a smile, Phil said, "We might be doing better here, then if we try do rob Orvald."

"Had the same thought myself," said Ralph. "The only problem we now have, how long can we keep stealing, and how long before someone notices, or recognize what we have as stolen merchandise? And Phil what will happen when someone does find out? What kind of punishment could we expect from the law enforcers? Will we spend time in the stockade, or will we lose our heads?"

"Yeah, I know Ralph. Whatever we do, we have our asses behind us, haven't we? We have enough products to stay with Orvald for a week, at least. Then if we want to continue with this trading, we have to start stealing more stuff." Said Phil in a matter of fact voice as he was shaking his head.

"Something wrong?" said Orvald. "You two, my friends, have had such a good day I would like to invite you to my own home. Would you be interested in sharing dinner with an old man?"

"Yeah, Orvald, that would be nice." Said Phil. "Of course, we would be interested, and we are thankful for the nice gesture. When do you want us to come over to your place?"

"No boys, when we are done here for the day, we pack down what we haven't sold, and we all together ride home to my place. It isn't that far away, and my housekeeper, Ranghild, an elderly woman, will have the food ready for us and she is good in the kitchen."

"Sounds too good to say no thanks," said Phil as the three started to clear the table. They put Orvald's merchandise in one basket, and their own in another. Then they put both basket on the cart Orvald used for his own selling.

Home at Orvald's place, there was plenty of space at the stable, and after they had taken care of the horses, they followed Orvald in to his house, it was even bigger than Trygg Bjornhild's house. In the kitchen, they saw this old woman. She must have been at least a hundred years old," thought Ralph as he together with Phil looked at her. Looking at Orvald, Phil said, "It isn't my business to ask. However, Orvald, how old is this woman that is looking after your home?"

"Her name is Ranghild, and she has been in my family's service since I was a little boy. My father was a year short of seventy when he died, he was a good well-behaved Viking, and Ranghild was with the family when my father was a young boy. Looking at the old woman, Orvald said. "Ranghild, do you know, or do you have an idea of your own age. How old you are?"

"Yes, master Orvald, I do. I was born before the first marauding Vikings disturbed our homes. I do believe I am ninety-seven years old. In another three years, I will be one hundred. And I will have beaten my own mother with five years of living." Said Ranghild as she brought out a heavy pot of stew, and put it on the table. "Did you make any money today Orvald?" she said as she put the ladle in the stew.

"Yes, Ranghild, together with these boys, I made more than I usually do on a Tuesday. If it was because of the boy's merchandise, drew more people to my table? I don't know. However,

Ranghild, even the boys did well, for whatever reason. Tomorrow, Wednesday, is usually the best weekday. But the weekend is always the best days for selling" said Orvald as he with a spoon put some of the stew in his mouth. And pointed at Bruce and Phil to help themselves.

Arriving at Count Drake's home, was a big surprise for both Helga and Loki. This wasn't a home, it was a castle, or a Palace, the most magnificent building either of them had ever seen. Helga looked with big eyes. "Is this really your home?"

"Yes Helga, it is my only home. You and my new friend Loki are welcome, not only as my guests, but as my personal friends. Those twenty odd Vikings would not only have stolen my new sword, and the money we together always have. They most probably would have taken my life as well. And as a thank you, to Loki, how can I show my gratitude? Or, even come close to what he did for me?"

"When you put it that way Count Drake, I can see

your problem." Said Helga as she unmounted her horse.

"This is for both of you, so please Loki Ragnarok listen to what I am telling you. I have only three personal friends in the whole world, you two have increased the number to five. You must from now, use my name Eirik when you talk to me, not Count Drake. Can we agree on that?"

"Yes, Eirik." Said Loki. "I would count it as a great favor to be among your personal friends. And to call you by the name Eirik, that your parents gave you when you were born, will be my pleasure. From now as you call me Loki, I'll call you Eirik, and I'll be proud of being counted as your friend." Said Loki as he helped Helga with her horse.

"That, without saying goes for me too," said Helga. "To be able to call you Eirik, is a privilege I take as a big favor." added Helga, as the three entered Eirik's home.

Before they had a chance to get inside, a loud scream was heard, and an arrow hit the wall right behind Loki. Far too close to where Helga was standing. Looking at the arrow, the three turned around, and saw the marauding Vikings were back to vengeance their dead friend.

"Let me borrow that sword again," said Loki, this time with an angry voice. "It seems to me, they have forgotten about Thor already. And to kill one of them wasn't enough. Had Helga moved a little bit faster, that arrow would have hit her body." With the sword in his right hand, Loki stood alone against at least twenty odd angry Vikings.

"Let's get him," shouted one of the Vikings, and as another arrow came flying, Loki stopped it easily with the sword.

"So, you came back for some more trashing?" he said with a loud voice as he stopped another arrow with the sword. As the Vikings were now on Count Drake's property, Loki moved forwards to meet them. The first couple of them, tried to turn around, or get away from Loki but the Vikings behind them kept on pushing. As soon as the first Vikings were only some yards from Loki, the air was again filled with Thor's voice. "Would you need some help brother?"

"No Thor, but thanks for asking," said Loki as he with the Counts sword killed the first two of the Vikings.

"Dad, I'm talking about Odin. He is giving you

your powers back even if you decide to stay with the people. Will be fun to see how a few Vikings can stand up to a fully powered man from Valhalla? Can you feel the powers arriving?" said Thor looking down at his brother.

"Yeah, Thor, it feels good. Give my thanks to Odin I have a feeling that our dragon Nidhug will get enough food today." With those words, Loki went through the Vikings like a thunder storm. It didn't take more than a few minutes, or maybe three, and the few Vikings still alive, started to run as fast as they could to their horses to get away from this mad-man. Fourteen of their friends were dead on the ground, and that person Loki stood there laughing with a well-tested sword in his hand. Not a drop of perspiration could be seen on his face, or his fore-head.

Eirik that had let Helga in to his house, to get her out of the danger zone. However, he wanted to see how Loki did with his new sword. It was with a big smile, he saw the few Vikings still alive running towards their horses, trying to escape the carnage.

Now it was time to look at Eirik's home. If this building looked beautiful from the outside, the inside looked marvelous. Helga couldn't get enough of what she saw. "Eirik, it must be nice to be able to live in a place like this. Did your parents live here when they were alive?"

"They are still alive Helga. They, both of them, live only a few miles from here. I visit them often, and they come to my home at least once every week. Please do come inside. I would like to offer you something, and then - - - I have to give you the two old swords for your dad Trygg, before I forget it."

Helga and Loki carefully entered this magnificent home. "Where have you found all these wonderful furniture's, and all the ornaments you have? As far as I know, no store in this country sells items like this." Said Helga as she carefully sat her behind down on a sofa that was softer, but still firm, than anything she had ever sat on.

"They come from different countries, mostly from Europe. When I was younger, my parents let me travel the world. The items I liked, I bought and they were sent here to my home." Said Eirik with a smile, and both Helga and Loki, could see on his face how proud he was.

"Now my new friends, let's have something to eat, and drink. My staff have the food ready, and I would be greatly honored if you Loki would join me and Helga for the needed food. Please come to my dinner table, and enjoy what you have greatly deserved." Said Eirik as he showed Loki and Helga where to sit.

The dinner, including the drinks were all well made, and Loki put in as much as he dared without being looked at. Helga, that didn't have the same body, didn't eat more than a lady should. As the three were enjoying the food, there was some high screams from outside. One of Eirik's servants, came and told him quietly that, "there are more Vikings outside, should I let them in?"

"Oh no James," said count Drake. "Loki Ragnarok will take care of the problem for us."

Loki stood up from the table, and with one of the count's old swords he went out to see what the trouble was. Coming out, there where an army of at least fifty Vikings on the counts property, and more by the forest further back.

"I can see you have got some of your friends together. Are you really sure another fight is what you want?" said Loki in a loud voice as he with a fast walk came closer to the marauding Vikings. As the last time, the once standing in front, tried to get away from Loki. However, the Vikings farther back pressed on.

Then, a loud voice came from the sky. Thor's voice came loud and clear. "This time Loki I would like to join in the fun." With those words, Thor was standing next to Loki. "You wouldn't have another sword, would you?" he said with his huge smile. "Thinking about it, I am much better with my own axe, and with its long handle I can reach further, so let's skip the sword."

"Sure, my brother. As far as I know there are at least another two swords in the house. Should I ask Helga to bring you one? But, as you said, I have seen you swing that axe, and if it makes you feel better, use it."

"Yeah, I might as well. For some reason, this group look like they really want a fight." Said Thor, as Helga opened the door, to let Thor use Eirik's new sword, but he shook his head, and showed her his axe. "I'm much faster with my axe, and with its long handle, I can kill more of the scum."

"You would have to be careful with this sword Thor, as it is count Drake's new one." She said as she gave the sword back to Eirik. She however, didn't go inside. Helga wanted to see the two brothers fight more Vikings than Loki first had counted, it was at least fifty fully armed Vikings standing ready to fight.

Looking towards his brother, Loki said. "Might need your help this time. Wonder where they found all the new fighters? Must be a new boat load of Vikings from one of their longboats. Well one thing is clear, our dragon will not go to bed hungry this day." With those words Loki and Thor went in between the Vikings, and Loki's sword, and Thor's axe killed more than they had ever killed before. It didn't take them a full five minutes, and the space between the Vikings grew larger.

"They are slowing down already?" said Loki as he with Eirik's old sword killed another Viking. There was now a good space between the Vikings, and they could fight better. "Look out for your back Thor," shouted Helga in a loud voice. They are coming from different directions. You have killed more than they were to start with. Where are the new once coming from?"

"It must be another group of Vikings trying to make a name for themselves. But they are thinning out, we have killed more than what is left fighting. I have a feeling we are on the winning side," said Thor. "However, my arm is getting tired. I'll use my hammer for a while." With those words, he took out the hammer and hit his right hand with it.

The effect was instant. The Vikings still fighting dropped their swords, and put their hands over their ears.

"No more!" screamed one of the leader of the larger group. "You from Valhalla have won, we will not fight the two of you any longer. You have proven that the two of you from Valhalla are stronger than all of us from Asgard. We will not fight you anymore. Is it possible for us regular Vikings to become your friends?" said this Viking that with a hand movement stopped the rest to fighting.

"Let's give it a chance," said Thor. "Might be that over time you from Asgard can prove yourselves as friends. Only time can tell" added Thor as he gave Helga a nod, and showed her his axe. And the three went back in to Eirik's home, for a well-deserved drink.

The end.

Printed in Great Britain
by Amazon